Star Dreams

Bernie—little blue-cream sister.

GROSSET & DUNLAP
Published by the Penguin Group
Penguin Group (USA) Inc., 375 Hudson Street, New York, New York 10014, USA
Penguin Group (Canada), 90 Eglinton Avenue East, Suite 700, Toronto,
Ontario M4P 2Y3, Canada
(a division of Pearson Penguin Canada Inc.)
Penguin Books Ltd., 80 Strand, London WC2R 0RL, England
Penguin Group Ireland, 25 St. Stephen's Green, Dublin 2, Ireland
(a division of Penguin Books Ltd.)
Penguin Group (Australia), 250 Camberwell Road, Camberwell, Victoria 3124, Australia
(a division of Pearson Australia Group Pty. Ltd.)
Penguin Books India Pvt. Ltd., 11 Community Centre, Panchsheel Park,
New Delhi—110 017, India
Penguin Group (NZ), 67 Apollo Drive, Rosedale, North Shore 0632, New Zealand
(a division of Pearson New Zealand Ltd.)
Penguin Books (South Africa) (Pty.) Ltd., 24 Sturdee Avenue,
Rosebank, Johannesburg 2196, South Africa

Penguin Books Ltd., Registered Offices:
80 Strand, London WC2R 0RL, England

Text copyright © 2006 Sue Bentley.
Illustrations copyright © 2006 Angela Swan.
Cover illustration copyright © 2006 Andrew Farley.
First printed in Great Britain in 2006 by Penguin Books Ltd.
First published in the United States in 2008 by Grosset & Dunlap,
a division of Penguin Young Readers Group, 345 Hudson Street,
New York, New York 10014. GROSSET & DUNLAP
is a trademark of Penguin Group (USA) Inc. Printed in the U.S.A.

Library of Congress Cataloging-in-Publication Data is available.

ISBN 978-0-448-45000-1   20 19 18 17 16 15

Star Dreams

SUE BENTLEY

Illustrated by Angela Swan

Grosset & Dunlap

★ Prologue ★

Flame heard a terrifying roar coming from nearby. He should have known it was too dangerous to come back home. His uncle Ebony was still looking for him.

Sparks crackled in Flame's fur and there was a flash of dazzling white light. A silky cream kitten with brown spots sat where the young white lion had stood just a moment ago.

An old gray lion appeared in the grass beside Flame. "Prince Flame! You shouldn't be here. You must hide!" the lion cried.

"There is no time, Cirrus," Flame meowed. "Uncle Ebony is almost here!"

Cirrus and Flame crouched down to hide in the grass. The ground shook as an enormous adult lion pushed through the grass. He stopped a foot away from Flame and Cirrus. The lion shook his mane and sniffed the air.

Flame's heart beat fast in his little body. He was sure the lion would see them hiding.

Finally, Ebony began to move away. He still sniffed the air in suspicion. "My nephew will never regain the throne. It is mine now! My spies will find him soon!" he said aloud.

Flame waited until Ebony was out of sight. He came out of hiding as his emerald eyes flashed with anger. "One day I shall rule, Cirrus!" he cried.

Cirrus smiled, revealing a row of worn teeth. "Indeed you will, Prince Flame. But first you must grow strong and powerful so you can fight your uncle. Use your kitten disguise and return now to the other world."

Silver sparks glittered in Flame's cream and brown fur as the tiny kitten felt the power building inside him. He said good-bye to Cirrus as he felt himself falling. The magic was working again . . .

Chapter
ONE

When Jemma Watson saw the new poster on the school bulletin board, she felt her heart beat faster.

Do you have what it takes to be a star? Auditions for places at A-One Dance School. Town Hall. Saturday, May 6. Everyone welcome.

Jemma did a quick account in her head. The auditions were the Saturday after next. Today was Thursday, so she had just over a week to get ready.

"Isn't it amazing! Are you going
for it?" asked an excited voice at her
shoulder. It was Fran Bradshaw, the
newest girl in Jemma's class.

Jemma knew that some of the
schoolkids thought Fran was a snob.
But she hadn't had the chance to get
to know her yet. Anyway, she liked to
make up her own mind about people.

She turned and smiled at Fran. "I
haven't decided yet. I don't know if I'd
be good enough."

"Me too. It's kind of scary, isn't it?" Fran said, her blue eyes wide.

Jemma grinned. She tossed her long brown hair over her shoulder. "Scary is a big hairy spider in the bathtub. Or telling Mr. Butler you didn't do your homework!"

Fran laughed. "You're right. So going for this audition is . . ."

"Terrifying!" Jemma said, rolling her eyes. She put her backpack on her shoulder and went toward the school exit with Fran. They passed the practice fields and tennis courts as they walked down the driveway. Beyond the front gates, Jemma could see lots of cars pulling up, ready to pick kids up and take them home.

"I've got an idea," Fran said. "Why

don't we practice our routines together? You could come to my house tonight. We can ask my mom. She's coming to

pick me up."

Jemma's spirits sank. She would love to accept Fran's invitation. "I can't tonight," she said reluctantly.

"Okay. What about tomorrow night? I could come to your house right after school, if you like."

"No!" It was out before Jemma could

stop herself. "Sorry. I mean, I'll have to let you know."

Fran gave her a puzzled look, but she shrugged. "Fine by me."

They had reached the school gate and Jemma saw Fran run over to a nice silver car. It had an open roof and fancy leather seats. It looked very expensive.

"Hi, darling," Mrs. Bradshaw called to her daughter. "Who's your new friend? Would she like a ride home?"

"Thanks, Mrs. Bradshaw, but it isn't far," Jemma called out quickly. "See you tomorrow, Fran!"

Jemma opened the worn front door and edged around the stroller and broken bike blocking the hall. She went into the kitchen.

"Hi, Mom," she called.

Mrs. Watson was cutting up potatoes. "Hi, sweetie. Good day at school?"

"It was okay," Jemma replied. She told her mom about the poster as she filled the sink with hot water and started washing the pile of breakfast dishes. "It's a great chance to get into dance school, isn't it? Can I go to the auditions?" she asked eagerly.

Mrs. Watson smiled. "I think you should. You are a wonderful dancer."

Jemma went over to give her a hug. "Thanks, Mom. I might practice with Fran Bradshaw, a new girl in my class. She's really nice."

Mrs. Watson patted her daughter's arm. "You should be spending more time with your friends, instead of helping out at home all the time."

"I don't mind," Jemma said, going across to her baby sister, Poppy, who sat in a high chair chewing her toast. Poppy gave Jemma a gummy grin.

"Hello, Poppy!" Jemma kissed her sister's fluffy blond head before going to the sink to fill the teapot. "I'll make us a cup of tea."

"Great! I've got just enough time for

one before I pick up the papers." Mrs. Watson had a paper route every night after she got home from her job at the supermarket. Sometimes Jemma helped her deliver the papers.

"Maybe you could ask Fran to come over sometime?" Mrs. Watson suggested.

Jemma glanced through the kitchen window at the tall weeds and blown-down fence. A picture of Fran's mom's expensive car came into her mind.

"I might," she said, but she knew she wouldn't.

A guilty feeling welled up inside her. Her mom was a single parent and she did the best she could, but Jemma sometimes got fed up with always having to make do.

"Bah, bah!" Poppy said, squashing

toast in her chubby hands.

"Same to you!" Jemma bent down
so that her face was level with her baby
sister's. Poppy was a happy little girl with
a sweet round face and big brown eyes.

"I'm going to go to an audition and
win a place in dance school. Yes, I am!"
Jemma said in a playful voice, so that
Poppy gurgled with laughter.

"Oh, yeah! Who says so?" shouted a
voice.

"Hi, Georgie!" Jemma didn't turn
around as her brother came crashing
through the back door. At eight years
old, he was two years younger than
Jemma. She heard the clunks as his soccer
shoes and then his backpack landed in a
heap on the floor.

"I'm starving! What's for dinner?"

demanded Georgie.

"It's not ready yet." Jemma straightened up and spun round. "Oh!"

Georgie stood there, grinning. There was mud all over his school pants. His white shirt was streaked with grass stains. And as for his face—Jemma could hardly see his freckles through all the spots of mud.

"What?" said Georgie, shrugging his shoulders.

Jemma couldn't understand how boys always get so messy. Put Georgie in a totally empty room and he'd come out looking like he'd been fighting with a dirt monster!

Mrs. Watson turned around. She shook her head slowly at Georgie. "Oh, my goodness! Look at you! You'd better

get changed and take a bath."

Georgie threw himself into a seat at the table. "Can't now. I'll pass out if I don't eat something."

Jemma grinned at her brother. "Milk and cookies okay?" She opened the fridge and took out the milk container. It was empty. "I'll have to go to the store. Keep an eye on Poppy while Mom's cooking," she told Georgie.

"Okay. But there's no way I'm

changing her," Georgie said with a mouthful of cookie.

Jemma asked her mom for some money, and then set off for Mr. Shah's shop. It took her a couple of minutes to walk to the end of the street and across the road. Mr. Shah sold all kinds of food and candy as well as newspapers and magazines. Jemma got the milk, then used the last of her money to buy a cherry cake that was on sale. They could all have it for dessert.

As she came out of the shop, something in the alley caught her eye. She stopped and stared at the garbage cans and piles of cardboard boxes. There it was again. A bright glow was coming from behind one of the cans.

Jemma frowned. She went into the

alley and bent down to look behind
the can. Confused, Jemma wondered
if it might be some kind of lamp that
someone had thrown away before the
batteries had run out.

Then the glow started to get brighter.
Whatever it was, was coming toward her!

Jemma almost dropped the milk. Two
bright emerald eyes stared at her in the
dark.

There was an angry hissing noise, and
suddenly Jemma realized what she was
staring at.

An enormous white lion crept slowly
out from behind the trash cans and
walked toward Jemma, his head held
high. A fountain of silver sparks fizzed
and crackled in the air around him.

Jemma froze in terror, her heart pounding. What was a lion doing here? Was he going to attack her?

"I am Prince Flame. Heir to the Lion Throne," growled the lion. "Who are you?"

"Whoa!" Jemma almost jumped out of her skin. He could talk!

Chapter
TWO

Panic clutched at Jemma's chest. She stood there in complete shock as Flame put his head to one side, waiting for an answer.

"I'm . . . er, Jemma. Jemma Watson. I live just around the corner," she stammered nervously. The amazing white lion's claws and teeth were very long and sharp.

Flame's eyes narrowed as he gave a satisfied smile. "Ah. You are a friend. Good," he purred.

There was a dazzling silver flash.

Jemma was blinded for a second.
She blinked hard and rubbed her eyes.
When she could see again, the lion had
disappeared. In his place was a cute
cream and brown kitten.

"What just happened?" Jemma gasped,
feeling some of the fear drain away. But
she still felt really weird about talking to
a cat. "Where's . . . Flame?"

"I am Flame," the kitten meowed. He had a pink nose, tiny paws, and fuzzy fur with brown spots.

"But how? Where's . . . ? What?" Jemma shook her head in confusion.

She must be dreaming. This was the Kingsley Estate, where she had lived all her life. Where the most exciting thing that happened was the annual garage sale behind the church. Glowing white lions just did not appear in alleys and then magically turn into cute kittens!

Flame took a wobbly step forward, and stood right in front of Jemma. He blinked up at her with scared, emerald-green eyes. "I need to hide. Jemma, can you help me?" he meowed urgently.

He looked so sweet and helpless. Leaning down, Jemma gently picked

Flame up and cuddled him. The kitten purred softly and his fur sparkled with hundreds of tiny silver lights.

Jemma felt a strange, prickly warmth against her palms. She wondered if Flame was going to transform again, but nothing happened. Suddenly, the sparks disappeared and Jemma's hands stopped tingling.

Flame reached up and touched Jemma's face with one tiny paw. "My enemies are searching for me. If they find me, they will kill me."

"What enemies? Who's after you?" Jemma asked.

"Uncle Ebony. He rules my kingdom. He has sent spies to take me back," replied Flame.

Jemma wanted to ask more about

Flame's world, but someone might come by at any minute and see them.

She made up her mind. "I'm taking care of you from now on. You're coming home with me." She zipped her jacket up around Flame. "Just wait until Georgie sees you!"

Flame stiffened. "You can't tell anyone that I am a prince!"

Jemma felt disappointed. Georgie would have loved to know about Flame, but she wasn't going to do anything that put him in danger.

"Okay. Don't worry. Your secret's safe with me," she said. With the milk and cake in one hand and Flame tucked under her arm, she went home.

"I'm sorry, but you know we can't afford pets, Jemma," Mrs. Watson said firmly, ten minutes later. "We'll call animal control. They'll find the kitten a good home."

"But Flame's special, Mom! He chose me to be his owner," Jemma said. *Oh, no, she didn't mean to say that! She had better be more careful.*

Luckily her mom just laughed. "You and your imagination, Jemma Watson!"

Jemma bit her lip. How could she change her mom's mind? She just *had* to let Flame live with them. He was in danger and she was the only one who could keep him safe. "Please, Mom. I'll take care of him. He can sleep in my room. And I'll buy his food with my allowance and everything."

"Slow down, sweetie. You know how you always rush into things," her mom said calmly.

"I know. But this is different," Jemma insisted. "Please, Mom."

"Oh, come on, Mom," urged Georgie, who was rolling a soft ball across the rug for Poppy to play with.

"I've thought of an awesome name for him . . . Fang."

"I don't think so!" Jemma screamed. She put on her best pleading voice. "Can Flame at least stay for tonight? Please?"

Her mom sighed and gave in. "I guess he can. But you have to put a flyer in the store window tomorrow. If an owner comes to claim him, there'll be no arguments."

"Thanks, Mom!" Jemma leaped out of the chair and gave her mom a hug.

"Can I feed Fang?" Georgie asked.

"Flame!" Jemma corrected her little brother again. Then her face fell. "We don't have any cat food. What's Flame going to eat?"

"Give him some milk for now, but too much isn't good for cats," Mrs.

Watson said. "You'd better get some cat food tomorrow, Jemma."

Jemma bit her lip. She just remembered that she had spent the last of her allowance on the cherry cake. How was she going to afford cat food?

Her mom seemed to know what she was thinking. She came over and put a couple of dollars in Jemma's hand. "That should hold you over until your next allowance."

"Thanks, Mom. You're the best!" Jemma said, beaming.

"Can I have some money, too?" Georgie piped up hopefully.

"You wish!" Jemma chuckled and ruffed her brother's sandy hair.

Once Flame had finished his milk, she took him upstairs. It was cozy in her bedroom with the evening sun pouring through the pink curtains. She scooped the blanket into a nest around the kitten. "There, how's that?"

Flame yawned, showing a tiny pink tongue and sharp white teeth. "Good.

I am warm now," he meowed sleepily.
"Jemma, will you keep my secret?"

"Cross my heart and hope to die,"
Jemma said. When Flame looked alarmed,
she giggled. "It means I promise not to
tell anyone," she said, petting his soft
ears.

Flame gave her a whiskery grin and
tucked his nose into his paws before
settling down to sleep.

Jemma sat on her bed beside him. A
bubble of happiness rose up from inside
her. "I can't believe this is happening!"
she breathed. "This is so cool!"

The following morning, Jemma woke
up to the sound of loud purring close to
her ear.

Rubbing her eyes, she sat up. She

went to bed late. She'd had to scribble a flyer about Flame for Mr. Shah's shop window and finish her homework. After that, she'd spent a long time trying to decide on a routine for the audition.

Flame uncurled himself. He stuck all four paws out and stretched his legs. "I slept well. I feel safe here," he meowed.

"You are safe with me!" Jemma said with a broad smile. She kissed the top of his soft little head.

Just then, the bedroom door flew open and Georgie exploded into the room. He leaped onto the bed and began playing with Flame.

"How are you, Fang?" he asked.

Jemma pushed her brother. "Ow! Get off, you big jerk, you're squashing me! And his name's not Fang!"

"Sausage!" Georgie said, using his word for "sorry." "Flame's a dumb name for a cat."

"No, it's not . . ." Jemma began. Suddenly she saw her clock. "Oh, no! We've overslept!" she groaned, throwing back the blanket. "Quick, Georgie. Go get dressed!"

When Georgie had gone out, Flame jumped off the bed and padded after

Jemma. "May I help?" he meowed.

"Thanks, Flame, but I'm fine."
Jemma's head was full of all the things
she had to do before school. She quickly
pulled on her uniform, and then dragged
a brush through her hair. Out in the
hallway she bumped into her mom.

Mrs. Watson was still in her nightgown.
Her hair was all messy and she looked
worried. "Oh, boy. I still have to iron my
uniform. I can't be late for work today.
We have staff training."

"Don't worry, Mom. I'll take care of
Poppy," Jemma offered.

"Thanks, sweetie," her mom said with
a relieved smile.

As Jemma went to the crib and picked
up her baby sister, Flame padded into
the room after her. He wrinkled his nose

and screwed up his face. "What is that bad smell?"

"It's just Poppy's diaper," Jemma said with a chuckle. "Come on, stinky little sis. You *really* need a bath!"

"Wa–ah!" Poppy had woken up in a bad mood. She screamed, yelled, and wriggled around, refusing to cooperate.

"Oh, not today, Poppy," Jemma pleaded as she filled the bathtub and undressed her sister. She lowered Poppy into the tub and splashed her with warm water. "I'm in a hurry. Be a good girl for me."

But Poppy stuck out her bottom lip and looked ready to scream. Jemma gritted her teeth and prepared for battle.

Suddenly she heard a crackling sound as silver sparkles shot out of Flame's fur. His green eyes began to glow like coals and his whiskers trembled with electricity. Jemma felt a tingling sensation. She caught her breath.

What was happening?

Chapter
THREE

Flame raised a paw and a fountain of silver sparks whooshed into the air.

Big, shiny, rainbow-colored bubbles appeared. They floated in the air, tinkling like silvery bells when they bumped gently into each other.

"Oooh!" Poppy squealed with delight, reaching her fat little hands up to catch the bubbles.

"Wow!" Jemma said. "That's awesome. How did you do that?"

Flame just smiled mysteriously, showing two sharp little teeth.

Poppy gurgled happily. Each time she grabbed a bubble, it burst into a cloud of purple, gold, or silver butterflies. They fluttered around the bathroom before gradually fading away.

"This is so much fun!" Jemma said, giggling as a small gold butterfly landed on the end of Poppy's nose and her little sister went cross-eyed looking at it.

"Why is everyone laughing? What's going on in there?" Jemma's mom called through the door.

"It's just Poppy playing with her bath toys!" Jemma called out. "Everything's fine."

She bit back another giggle as Flame gently tapped a huge purple butterfly with his front paw and it turned into a shower of tiny silver sparks.

"There, finished!" Jemma said, buttoning Poppy's tiny soft shoes after they had dressed her. Downstairs, she put Poppy in her playpen with some toys before going into the hall to grab her school books.

Flame followed, watching everything curiously. Just then, Jemma saw Georgie's enormous plastic lunch box sticking up out of his backpack.

She groaned. "Oh, no! His sandwiches! He takes tons of them or he complains he's hungry all day at school. Mom must have forgotten. I'll have to make some now—I'm going to be so late!"

Flame's ears pricked. "I will help!"

His fur began to sparkle again and his whiskers crackled. Jemma felt the familiar hot tingling down her spine. Flame lifted a paw and a spray of green light shot toward the lunch box.

Jemma went over and peeped through the clear plastic lid. She saw piles of ham and cheese sandwiches, cookies, and lemonade. "All of Georgie's favorites! Thanks, Flame!" she said delightedly.

"You are welcome," meowed Flame, looking pleased with himself.

There was a knock at the door. It was Georgie's school friends. Georgie raced downstairs, grabbed his bag, and raced out of the front door. "Bye, Jems. Later!" he shouted.

"Bye, Georgie!" Jemma replied with a grin.

Mrs. Watson gave her a quick hug as she left on her way to take Poppy to day care. "Bye, Jemma. Thanks for being such a big help this morning. Have a good day at school."

Jemma pulled on her school coat and grabbed her bag. "Bye, Flame. See you when I get home. Be good!" she joked, dropping a quick kiss on the kitten's head.

Flame gave her a strange, secret smile and began washing his ears.

Fran Bradshaw was waiting at the school gate when Jemma arrived.

"Hi. Did you decide which song you're going to dance to?" she asked Jemma.

"What?" Jemma said, looking blank.

"Hello? The auditions for A-One Dance School—remember?" Fran brushed a strand of hair out of her eyes.

"Oh, *that* song!" Jemma remembered. "I have a couple I'm thinking about, but I'm not sure which I like best." She wondered what Fran would say if she told her she'd been running around that morning, helped by a magic kitten!

Jemma felt the excitement rising in her again as Fran talked about the auditions. It surprised her how badly she wanted to win a spot at the school. She loved being on stage.

"I was thinking about working on my routine during lunch. Would you mind helping me with some moves?" Fran asked.

Jemma was glad to help, and anyway, it would be fun. "Sure. I'd love to. I could meet you by the soccer fields," she replied.

"Okay, great!" Fran said, her blue eyes shining.

They walked into class together. Fran sat at the back and Jemma took her usual seat by the window. But as Jemma reached into her bag for her books, she gasped.

There was something warm and furry in the bag, too.

Georgie! she thought. *It was one of his tricks.* But as Jemma touched it, the furry ball began purring.

Oh, no! Flame! What was he doing here?

Jemma looked around to see if anyone was watching, and then put her face close to her bag. "You can't come to school, Flame!" she whispered. "We're not allowed to bring pets!"

"What is a pet?" Flame asked.

"It's . . . er, an animal friend. People

own them," Jemma hissed.

"I am not a pet!" said Flame indignantly.

Jemma frowned. "No, you're not. But you're still not allowed to come here."

Flame didn't seem to grasp this logic. Suddenly his face brightened. "I will stay. Do not worry! I will use my magic, so that only you may see me at school."

"You mean, you can make yourself invisible just while you're here? Hey, that's cool!" She still wasn't sure about Flame being at school with her. It could lead to all kinds of problems. But it was too late to do anything about it now.

"Jemma Watson, would you like to tell us all what's so interesting about your backpack?" a sarcastic voice called out.

Mr. Butler, her class teacher, had

messy brown hair. He had a way of looking over his glasses when he was annoyed.

"Er . . . Nothing, sir," Jemma said quickly, sitting straight back up.

"Then perhaps I could have your full attention," Mr. Butler drawled.

"Yes, sir." Jemma felt her cheeks turn

red as the rest of the class laughed.

There was a soft thump beside her as Flame jumped out of her backpack. He walked across her desk and went and sat on a windowsill.

No one noticed.

So it's true, Jemma thought. *While he's at school with me, only I can see him.* She decided to relax and concentrate on her schoolwork.

The morning passed quickly. Now and then Jemma caught sight of Flame. Once, he was sitting right next to Mr. Butler, looking over the teacher's shoulder. She smiled, wondering if magic kittens could read. Later, she saw him outside chasing bees in the flower beds around the tennis courts.

At lunchtime, Jemma and Fran went

out to the soccer fields. It was a warm day and lots of other kids were sitting around on the grass. She could see Georgie and a group of his friends some distance away. *I bet he's enjoying his lunch*, she thought.

Fran stood up. "I've started working on a routine. Should I show you what I've done so far? This is the beginning." She struck a pose, sidestepped, did a dip, and then a twirl.

"Mmm," Jemma said. "It's okay, but I think you could make it more exciting."

Fran frowned. "I thought that, too. What should I do?"

"How about this?" Jemma demonstrated some steps. "Now you try."

Fran followed Jemma's moves. Both girls were giggling at Fran's first few attempts, but after a few minutes she had them down. "That's great! Thanks, Jemma. It's much better now."

"It will be even better when we do our routines to music," Jemma said.

Fran nodded. "I can't wait. I've been thinking about my costume. We could go into town and buy them together. Mom says she'll take us."

"Oh, um, right." Jemma's heart sank. She had planned to wear something she already had. She knew her mom couldn't afford new clothes.

Just then Jemma heard shouting and whoops of laughter. She turned around and saw some kids running toward Georgie and his friends.

"What's going on?" Fran asked. "Is it a fight?"

Jemma groaned. It looked like Georgie

was up to something, as usual. "It's my brother. I'd better find out what he's up to. Come on!" She took off running.

Jemma and Fran bounded across the grass. At first Jemma couldn't see Georgie through the crowd of kids around him. She pushed her way through them.

"Oh!" gasped Jemma.

Georgie stood there, a look of delighted amazement on his freckled face. He was holding his open lunch box in two hands. Shooting out of it was a multicolored volcano of sandwiches, potato chips, cookies, and candy!

Chapter
FOUR

Jemma stared in dismay at the growing
mountain of sandwiches and candy.

Georgie was already up to his knees
in chocolate cookies and cherry cakes.
"There's lots more. Help yourselves!" He
chewed happily, his cheeks bulging.

Flame's spell must be out of control.
The magic lunch box showed no signs of
slowing down.

"Where's it all coming from?" Fran
said, frowning.

"I . . . er . . . don't know," Jemma
lied, trying to buy time.

Everyone was collecting up food and
roaring with laughter. One of Georgie's
friends was making a tower of peanut
butter and jelly sandwiches. Another was
juggling with coffee cakes. Two more
boys were skimming lemon candies across
the grass.

I have to find Flame, thought Jemma.
He's the only one who can undo the magic.

But where was he? She spun

around, slowly scanning every inch of the soccer field. There was a tiny figure bounding around in the grass.

It was Flame. He was playing with two enormous pigeons.

Somehow she had to get his attention. But before she could decide what to do, she heard an angry shout. Turning around, she saw a figure striding across the soccer field toward her.

"Mr. Butler," she groaned.

"What on earth is going on here?" Mr. Butler's sharp eyes spotted Georgie. "George Watson, is that you? I might have known," he snapped, peering over his glasses.

"It's not Georgie's fault!" Jemma leaped to her brother's defense.

Mr. Butler turned around and faced her.

"Then perhaps you can tell me who *is* responsible for this mess, young lady?" he demanded.

Jemma opened her mouth to answer and then shut it again. She couldn't tell her teacher about Flame, and anyway, she doubted if he would believe her.

She sent out a silent cry for help. *Oh, Flame, please come over here and undo your spell.*

"I want this stopped—now! Pick up those sandwiches. And you, get a bag to put those cookies in!" Mr. Butler barked orders to the grinning schoolkids.

"Food fight!" someone yelled. The other boys took up the chant. "Food fight! Food fight!"

With a glint in his eye, Georgie grabbed a cherry cake and aimed it.

"Georgie! Don't you dare . . ."
warned Jemma.

But it was too late. *Splat!* The cherry
cake hit Mr. Butler in the chest. *Squish!*
Another cake hit his glasses. The teacher's
face reddened with anger and he gave
a roar of rage. An enormous chocolate
eclair torpedoed into his open mouth
as one boy with particularly good aim
looked very proud of himself.

Suddenly cakes and sandwiches were
hurtling everywhere. Jemma ducked and
backed away. Georgie, his friends, and
Mr. Butler began to disappear beneath
layers of jam, cookies, and cream.

Fran was trying hard not to laugh. "I
wouldn't want to be in Georgie's shoes!"
she gasped.

"He'll probably be grounded for the

entire semester!" Jemma said. "Mom's
going to be furious!" Just then, she felt a
small furry body rub against her leg. She

glanced down with relief. "Flame! Am I
glad to see you!" she whispered.

"My magic is too strong! I will fix it,"
he meowed.

As silver sparks fizzed around Flame,
Jemma felt her spine tingle. Flame lifted
a paw and a spray of purple glitter shot

toward the food fighters. There was a puff of smoke and all the food disappeared, down to the very last ham sandwich!

For a couple of seconds, no one moved.

Jemma grabbed Fran's sleeve. "Quick! Run, before old Butler starts asking more questions." Fran stumbled behind her.

As they reached the school, Jemma burst out laughing. "I'll never forget old Butler's face when that eclair zoomed into his mouth!"

Fran stopped. She shook her head and then looked at Jemma, her face blank. "When? What do you mean?" she asked.

"You know . . . just now . . . old Butler . . ." Jemma paused, looking puzzled. Fran obviously had no idea what she was talking about!

Other kids were sauntering back
toward the school. Georgie and his
friends were walking along, chatting with
each other. Mr. Butler was striding along
calmly behind them. Jemma frowned.

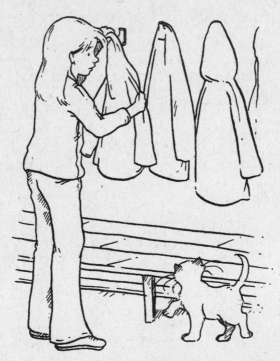

How come everyone was suddenly acting as if nothing unusual had happened?

In the coatroom, Jemma heard a sheepish meow at her feet. She looked down to see Flame. "Sorry, Jemma. I used my magic so that no one would remember what took place."

Jemma laughed with relief. So that's why everyone was acting so normal!

After checking that no one was looking, she gave Flame a quick cuddle.

Chapter
FIVE

The next day was Saturday. Fran called first thing in the morning.

"Can you come over to my house?" she asked Jemma. "I'm dying to work on our routines."

"I'd love to, but I can't right now," Jemma said. Someone had called out sick at the supermarket and Mrs. Watson had to work all day. Jemma was babysitting Poppy.

"Oh," Fran said. "Are you doing anything interesting?"

Jemma bit her lip. It was too

embarrassing to explain that you had
to look after your baby sister. "I'm just
really busy. Sorry."

"It's okay. Maybe another time," Fran
said and hung up.

Jemma sighed. She felt awful. She
could tell Fran was disappointed.

Jemma gave Poppy her breakfast,
bathed her, and got her dressed. "Let's go
to the park and see Georgie. He's playing
soccer with his friends."

Poppy gurgled happily as Jemma

lifted her into her high chair. She loved Georgie.

Flame had been stretched out on a windowsill, enjoying the sun. He pricked up his ears at the promise of an outing. "May I come, too?"

Jemma patted the stroller. "Hop on and I'll give you a ride," she said with a grin.

Flame jumped up, and much to Poppy's delight, settled himself on the folded rain hood, purring loudly. Jemma wheeled Poppy into the street and they set off for the park.

It was a hot day and there were lots of people on the swings and jungle gym.

Jemma spotted Georgie and his friends kicking a ball around over near the slide.

Jemma parked the stroller in the shade beneath a tree and gave Poppy a bottle of fruit punch. Flame climbed up the trunk and stretched out lazily on a branch. Jemma smiled. He was enjoying looking down on the world.

On the other side of the park, she noticed some girls by the tennis courts. They all had expensive rackets and wore nice outfits.

Jemma would have loved to be able to wear clothes like that and join in the game. One of the best-dressed girls looked over and waved.

It was Fran.

Jemma waved back, her heart sinking. She wished she wasn't wearing her oldest T-shirt and jeans and running around after her brother and sister. But it was too late to make a getaway now. Fran was coming over.

"Hi, Jemma!" Fran ran up, beaming, her fair hair flying out behind her. "I

saw Georgie playing soccer with his friends and wondered if you were here. Is this your little sister?" Fran bent down in front of the stroller. She wiggled her finger so that Poppy gave her a gummy grin.

Jemma nodded. "Her name is Poppy." She had been worried that Fran might be upset at finding her in the park after she had made an excuse not to go to her house. But she was surprised and happy that Fran seemed cool about it.

Fran smiled. "Isn't Poppy adorable? You're so lucky to have a brother and sister."

"Do you think so?" Jemma said, surprised.

Fran nodded. "Everyone thinks it's great to be an only child, because you get spoiled and everything. But I've always wanted a brother or sister to share things with."

"Oh," Jemma murmured. She had never thought of it that way. "Well, you can share mine. Georgie's enough trouble for two families!" she joked.

Fran laughed. "Do you have to babysit

Poppy and Georgie tomorrow?"

"No. Mom's at home. I could come over to your house, if that's okay," Jemma said.

Fran's face lit up. "Awesome! I've been working on my routine, but I need a lot more practice. Well—I'd better get back to my friends now. See you tomorrow!" She reached down to kiss Poppy's cheek. "Bye, Poppy. Be good!"

As Fran went off to play tennis, Georgie ran over. "I'm dying of thirst!" He grabbed a drink from under the stroller. "What did that rich girl want?"

"Don't call her that. Fran's all right," Jemma told him.

Sunday afternoon was bright and sunny.

Jemma and Fran were in Fran's bedroom. It was a big room with lots of posters on the walls. Jemma gently lifted Flame out of her bag and put him on the floor.

"I thought you might like to meet my new friend," she said.

"Oh, he's so sweet! He's such a pretty color." Fran admired Flame's cream coat with its brown spots.

Flame gave a friendly meow and walked over to Fran.

"He likes you. Would you like to hold him while I show you my routine?" Jemma asked.

Fran nodded eagerly. She lifted Flame into her lap and then sat cross-legged on her bed, watching as Jemma danced in time to the beat.

"Ta-dah!" Jemma froze in her final pose, just as the music stopped. "How did that look?"

Fran jumped up and clapped her hands. "That was really good!"

Flame gave a soft yowl of approval.

Fran laughed. "Flame agrees with me!"

Jemma performed a mock bow. "Thanks, fans," she joked. "All I have to do now is polish up my moves."

"Piece of cake. Not!" Fran made a face.

They heard footsteps on the stairs. Fran's mom came into the room with a tray. "How's it going in here? I thought you might like a drink and a snack." She noticed Flame and gave him a friendly pat.

"Thanks, Mrs. Bradshaw." Jemma

helped herself to some juice and a
chocolate cookie.

"Jemma's really good, Mom," Fran
said generously.

Jemma blushed. "I'm not bad."

"You'll have to get your costumes
organized. Have you decided when
you want to go into town?" asked Mrs.
Bradshaw.

"Not yet," Jemma said quickly, feeling anxious. The friendly reminder made her realize that she really had to decide what to wear.

Mrs. Bradshaw smiled. "Well—just let me know."

After a short break, Fran put her music on and she and Jemma worked on some more steps. When they were tired of practicing, Fran pulled a box of magazines from under the bed and they stretched out together on a colorful rug to read them.

Flame curled up with them and began playing with a loose thread hanging out of the rug.

Jemma was really enjoying herself with Fran, but when she glanced at her watch she was shocked to see how late it was. She leaped to her feet and grabbed her bag. "I have to go now! Jump in, Flame."

Fran saw her to the front door. "See you tomorrow at school. Don't forget what Mom said about our costumes. We've got less than a week before the auditions," she reminded her excitedly.

"Oh, er, right." Jemma's good mood began to fade.

She didn't see Flame looking up at her, a thoughtful look in his green eyes.

What is the point of kidding myself, Jemma thought. She couldn't afford new clothes and there was no way she was going in for the audition in some ugly old costume. Maybe she should just tell Fran she was dropping out.

Chapter
SIX

"You're quiet, sweetie," Mrs. Watson said as she wiped the kitchen table that evening. "Is something wrong?"

Jemma sighed as she ran the iron over her school shirt. Flame was napping on a kitchen chair beside her. "I don't think I'll bother going to the audition," she said, trying to sound as if she didn't mind.

Her mom stopped dead and looked at her in surprise. "But Jemma, you were so excited! Did something happen?"

Jemma shrugged. "Not really. I . . . I

just changed my mind."

Mrs. Watson frowned. She dried her hands before coming over and putting her arm around Jemma. "Come on. Tell me," she said gently.

Jemma's worries started to spill out, and once she started she couldn't stop. "It's just that I don't have anything to wear. Fran's going to get a new costume, and I bet everyone else will, too, except me! I'm going to really stand out and

look stupid in front, of all my friends!"
She hung her head. "I didn't want to
tell you, Mom. I know we can't afford
to buy anything new. Anyway, it doesn't
matter now. I've made up my mind. I'm
not going to the audition."

"Hmm." Mrs. Watson looked
thoughtful. She opened a kitchen cabinet
and took out a cup. "Would this help
to change your mind?" she said, pressing
some money into Jemma's hand.

"But that's for your winter coat.
You've been saving for it for so
long!" Jemma looked at her mom in
amazement.

"There's still time to save up again.
You need a costume and we're going to
get you one," Mrs. Watson said firmly.

Jemma gave her mom a huge hug.

"You're the best mom in the world!"

Flame sat up suddenly and began purring loudly. He gave Jemma and her mom a wide, catty grin.

"I know it sounds strange, but I think that kitten understands every word we say," Mrs. Watson said with a chuckle.

Jemma smiled to herself, but said nothing.

"Be careful you don't fall!" Jemma said to Flame as she walked down the street swinging her backpack on Wednesday.

"I am fine, thank you, Jemma," meowed Flame happily as he tiptoed across the tops of fences and garden gates, keeping up with Jemma.

His ears were pricked and his tail stuck up. The sunlight made the brown spots on his cream fur really stand out.

"I can't wait until I see Fran," Jemma said to him. "We can go into town and buy our costumes together now!"

Flame purred in agreement. He batted at a bumblebee and almost lost his balance.

Jemma giggled and reached out to steady him. Just then, someone came barging around the corner and knocked right into her.

Jemma stumbled and almost fell over. "Hey!" she called angrily at the back of the stocky figure, who kept on walking right past her.

"What?" He turned around and came back. Jemma recognized him now. It was Sam Thomas, a tough boy from their school who picked on some of the younger children—even Georgie sometimes.

"Uh-oh," she murmured.

"Well, if it isn't that freckly kid's sister," Sam scoffed. "Is that your kitten? What a flea bag!"

Before Jemma realized what was happening, Sam reached out and grabbed Flame by the scruff of his neck. As the boy pulled him off the fence, Flame meowed with alarm. His body just hung there, and his legs and tail dangled down.

He was helpless.

"Stop it! Put him down!" Jemma fumed.

"Let's see if he can fly!" Sam pretended to throw Flame over a nearby garden wall.

Flame gave a terrified wail. His paws

clawed at the air. He seemed too scared to do any magic. Or maybe he didn't want to give himself away.

Jemma's stomach clenched. "Please don't hurt him!" she begged.

Sam lifted his hand slowly, higher and higher, ready to throw Flame into the air.

He's really going to do it, Jemma thought. She felt desperate. She had to help Flame. But what could she do?

"Wait!" she cried. Plunging her hand into her pocket, she took out her costume money and showed it to Sam. "Let him go and I'll give you this."

Sam's eyes lit up greedily. He reached for the money.

Jemma snatched back her hand. "Give

me Flame first," she demanded. Her knees were shaking, but she made herself stare boldly at the mean older boy.

Sam made up his mind. "Here. Have your stupid kitten."

He thrust Flame at Jemma and grabbed the money. Without looking back, he went on his way.

Jemma's hands trembled as she cuddled Flame. The thought of him being hurt gave her a horrible sick feeling. "I've got you. You're safe now," she said softly.

Flame dug in with his claws and clung
tightly to her school shirt. He looked up
at her with round, troubled eyes.

"Jemma, all your money is gone," he
whimpered.

"It doesn't matter," she told him,
rubbing her chin on his soft head.

She tucked Flame into her backpack, where he curled up next to her pencil case. She kept her hand in her bag, petting him gently until he began to purr.

Jemma grew calmer as she walked to school, but her spirits were low.

There was no way she could tell her mom that the money had been stolen. And her last chance of buying a costume for the audition was gone for good.

The school day seemed to pass by in a blur. Jemma's class was doing medieval history, but Jemma just couldn't concentrate. How was she going to enter the audition without a costume?

At least Flame seemed okay after his ordeal. Jemma had to smile. She watched

Flame jumping around the classroom
from desk to desk. He seemed very
interested in the open medieval history
books. Once, she saw him staring at a
computer screen, dabbing at the keyboard
with his paw.

Jemma hurried home when school
finished. It was her mom's late night
at the supermarket. She planned to get
dinner ready for when she came home.

Just as she let herself into the house,
she heard a crash.

"Oh, heck!" shouted a voice.

"Georgie! Is that you?" Jemma called.
He was supposed to be playing with a
friend after school.

Georgie stuck his head around the
kitchen door. There was flour all over
his face and his hair stuck up in white

powdery spikes. "Hi, Jems!" he said brightly. "I came straight home. I've got a surprise for you. I'm making dinner!"

Jemma had a strange sinking feeling. She slowly pushed open the kitchen door.

Flour covered the table and the floor. White footprints trailed all through the house. Sticky red fingerprints smeared the wall, the fridge, and the oven.

"Pizza!" said Georgie proudly.

Jemma was speechless.

Mom was going to go crazy!

"In the shower—now!" she ordered Georgie.

He scowled, but did as she told him.

She dashed toward the closet and took out the vacuum cleaner. Plugging it in, Jemma switched it on. There was a loud

bang and a puff of black smoke.

The vacuum cleaner had died.

"Oh, that's just great!" Jemma cried
out. She felt like bursting into tears.
She'd had a horrible day and it wasn't
getting any better.

There was a shower of sparks as Flame
jumped onto the kitchen table. "I will
help," he meowed.

Jemma felt the warm, magical tingling
and wondered what was going to happen

next.

A minute later, the vacuum cleaner burst into action. It zoomed around wildly, making clean trails through the flour. "Must clean up! Must clean up!" it hummed, rolling into the living room.

"Wow! Thanks, Flame," Jemma said. She grabbed a cloth and began scrubbing at a tomato sauce fingerprint. Her mom would be home soon. With a little luck, she might have time to clean up this mess.

Just then she heard the vacuum cleaner give a loud cough, and then it burped.

Jemma stood in the doorway, staring in horror at the scene before her. The vacuum cleaner wove back and forth, sucking up everything in its path. It swallowed a pile of books and a shirt, and began chomping the curtains.

"Oh, heck!" Jemma gasped. It looked like the vacuum was going to gobble up the whole room!

There was a faint sound above the noise. Jemma's head came up. It was the front door closing.

Mom was home!

Chapter
SEVEN

"Flame! Do something!" Jemma wailed.

Flame's whiskers crackled as he lifted a paw. A comet's tail of gold sparks flew all around the room.

Bang! The vacuum cleaner whizzed back into the closet. *Swish!* Cushions, carpets, and curtains flicked back into place. *Phloop!* Flour and sauce disappeared back into bags and jars.

Mrs. Watson came into the kitchen, carrying Poppy.

"Hi, Mom," Jemma said breathlessly.

"Did you have a good day?"

"Not bad," her mom said, smiling. "My goodness! You and Georgie have been busy. Everything's sparkling clean. And what's that cooking?" She opened the oven door. "A pizza? Great."

Jemma grinned at her mom. "Georgie made the pizza. With a bit of help!" *And a big dose of magic*, she thought.

Jemma went straight up to her bedroom after dinner, before her mom started asking questions about when she was going to buy her costume. She wanted to put off telling her about the money for as long as she could.

Flame followed her into the room. He rubbed himself against her legs. "Do you need a costume?" he meowed.

Jemma nodded sadly. "Yes, I do. But it's not going to happen, is it?"

Flame tilted his head to one side. His tail stuck up. A couple of sparks flicked out of the end. "Close your eyes!" he meowed eagerly.

Despite herself, Jemma smiled. What was he up to? She closed her eyes. A familiar tingling spread all over her.

"Look now!" Flame told her.

Slowly, Jemma opened her eyes. Her jaw dropped as she stared at her reflection. "Oh, my goodness," she gasped.

She wore a long dress of yellow silk and bright-red velvet. It had a V-neck and long sleeves. On her head there was a tall, pointed hat with a floaty veil.

Flame had made her a medieval

costume! Jemma's heart sank. Flame must have gotten the idea from one of her classmate's textbooks at school that day.

"Do you like it?" Flame asked proudly, his tail in the air.

"It's . . . um . . . beautiful," she stammered. "But I can't wear it for the audition. How would I dance in it?"

Flame looked dejected. "Is the dress wrong, Jemma?"

"No, not at all," Jemma said quickly, not wanting Flame to feel bad. She bent down to pet him. "I love it. Really, I do. I'll keep it for a costume party," she promised. "Thanks, Flame."

"You are welcome!" Flame cheered up.

He gave her a whiskery grin. Jumping back onto the bed, he began licking his fur.

"Jemma! Could you come down here, please?" her mom called up the stairs.

"Coming, Mom!" Jemma quickly took off the dress and put it in her closet.

She found her mom in the hall, filling a bag with books. "I just remembered these library books. They're due back today. Be a good girl and take them for me, will you? The library's open until seven P.M."

"Okay." Jemma checked the time. It was already 6 P.M. "I'll go now."

It took only a few minutes to walk to the library. She handed the books in and still had time to look around.

In the children's section, there was a rack of magazines. Jemma chose one and spread it open on a table. It had pictures of rock stars, a puzzle page, and tons of stuff about makeup and hairstyles.

As she flipped a page, she saw a photo of a girl in a red T-shirt decorated with bright ribbons, buttons, and sequins. It looked really expensive and it was just the type of thing Jemma would have loved to have worn.

As Jemma closed the magazine, a brilliant idea jumped into her head. That was it! Her problem was solved. But would Fran agree with her?

Jemma called Fran the minute she got home. She told her about the photo of the gorgeous T-shirt. "Why don't we make our own costumes? It can't be that hard. We've already got jeans and T-shirts. And my mom's great at sewing. I could ask her to help us!"

"And no one else would have anything like them!" Fran got caught up in the excitement. "My mom's got a big box of sewing stuff. It's got ribbons and sequins and tons of other things in it. I'll ask her if we can use some of that."

"Great!" Jemma said, then she bit her lip. "Tomorrow is Thursday. The auditions are on Saturday!"

There was a short silence before Fran

replied. "We can do this! But we'll have to work on them Thursday and Friday night. How about if I come to your house right after school?"

Jemma hesitated. She still felt doubtful about letting Fran see her messy house. Then she remembered how friendly and relaxed Fran had been with Poppy.

"Okay. I'll tell my mom," she decided. "I'm sure she won't mind. But we'll have to think of something to keep Georgie out of the way!"

Fran chuckled. "Leave it to me!"

With Fran coming over, Jemma decided she was going to have to tell her mom what happened to the costume money.

She went into the living room where Mrs. Watson was on the sofa reading the local newspaper. Jemma sat down next to her. "Mom, I've got something to . . ." she stopped in surprise as she saw a familiar name in the paper. "That's Sam Thomas, from my school! Why is he in the paper?"

"Apparently an old couple caught him stealing apples from their back garden," her mom told her. "The old lady chased

Sam with her walking stick and he fell backward into their garden pond. Her husband took a photo as Sam tried to climb out. Do you know this boy?"

Jemma nodded. "Sam Thomas is really mean. A lot of kids are scared of him." She told her mom about bumping into the older boy on the way to school. "Sam threatened to throw Flame over a garden wall. I thought he was going to do it. So I gave him the money for my costume to stop him. I'm really sorry for losing the money, Mom, but I didn't know what else to do."

There was a long pause, and then Mrs. Watson sighed. "I'd probably have done the same thing if I was in your shoes." She slipped her arm around her daughter's shoulders. "I bet you've been worrying about this, haven't you? You should have come and told me right away."

"I know," Jemma said, feeling better for having gotten it off her chest. "Next time I will!"

"Good." Suddenly Mrs. Watson began laughing. "Look at this! I'd say that bully got what he deserved, wouldn't you? This

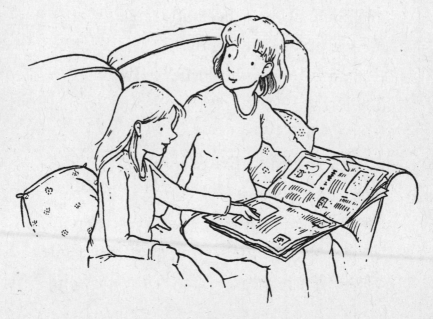

will be all over your school tomorrow!"

She opened the newspaper so that Jemma could see the picture of Sam Thomas crawling out of the muddy pond with weeds piled on his head and dripping from his ears. The old lady stood there, waving her stick at him.

"He doesn't look so tough now, does he?" Jemma burst out laughing as she imagined all the schoolkids seeing the picture of the mean boy.

Sam Thomas would never live it down.

On Thursday, Fran's mom gave Jemma and Fran a ride home. "Don't forget this! And these." She passed Fran the big box full of sewing stuff and a pile of soccer magazines. "Have fun, girls. I'll pick you up later, Fran. Bye!" She drove away.

Georgie's eyes lit up when he saw the magazines. "I borrowed them from our next-door neighbor," Fran explained with a grin.

Jemma chuckled. They would keep him quiet for hours. Now they could get on with sewing without Georgie "helping."

It was Mrs. Watson's half-day. She had dinner ready. Afterward, Jemma and Fran cleared a space on the kitchen table and spread out their T-shirts.

Fran sorted through her mom's old sewing stuff. "Wow! Look at this sparkly ribbon. I love these pink sequins."

Jemma chose some colorful ribbons and glittery purple beads. As Jemma and

Fran set to work, helped by Jemma's mom, Flame wandered into the kitchen. He meowed a greeting.

"Hello again, Flame," Fran said.

"Did you have a nice nap?" Jemma got up and poured some dry cat food into a bowl.

Flame gobbled it up, purring loudly.

"Isn't he cute? Like a ball of brown and cream fluff with big green eyes!" Fran admired Flame. "When did you get him?"

"He hasn't lived here for long. But it feels like I've always had him," Jemma said. It was difficult to even imagine life without Flame now.

A few hours later, the T-shirts were looking good, but there was still a lot of work to do. And they hadn't even started on their jeans.

"Fran's mom will be here soon,"
Mrs. Watson said. "I think it's time you
stopped for now. Tell me what you
want me to do and I'll work on it for a
while."

"Thanks, Mom," Jemma said
gratefully. Her fingers were starting to
hurt from all the hand sewing.

Fran's mom arrived and Jemma waved
to her friend as the car pulled away.
There was just enough time to practice
her routine before she went to bed.

The next day at school, she and Fran
grabbed every spare moment to practice
their dance moves. They did their
routines in the hallway between classes
and even ate lunch while dancing.

"Maybe I should add this move to
my routine!" Fran joked, posing with a

sausage roll in one hand and a box of orange juice in the other.

"Definitely! It's a real winner!" Jemma said, giggling.

Right after school, they went back to Jemma's house and began sewing.

"Your mom's amazing!" Fran held up her jeans. The pockets and hems glittered with beads and sequins.

"Yes, she is," Jemma agreed. Her jeans had seams decorated with silver and purple beads. Mrs. Watson had even made a matching belt of braided ribbons.

By the time Fran had to go, their costumes were finished. Jemma hoped she'd never set eyes on another needle and thread! But she had to admit, the costumes looked amazing.

"Tomorrow's the big day!" Jemma

said to Flame as he snuggled up beside her on the bed.

She was sure she wouldn't sleep a wink. But she fell asleep the moment her head hit the pillow.

On Saturday morning, Jemma could hardly concentrate on helping her mom deliver papers. She felt nervous but excited. In just a few hours she would be performing her routine in front of a panel of judges.

Back at home, Mrs. Watson made
a quick sandwich but Jemma was too
nervous to eat anything.

"Sit here, sweetie, so I can do your
hair," her mom said. She brushed,
pinned, and sprayed Jemma's long brown
hair and then carefully applied some stage
makeup.

Jemma looked at herself in a mirror.
"It looks great, Mom. Thanks!"

She went upstairs to her bedroom,
folded her costume carefully, and put it
in a bag. Flame was stretched out on the
windowsill, soaking up the sun.

"It's time to go and meet Fran,"
Jemma said to him.

"Can I come, too?" he meowed,
jumping down.

Jemma gave him a quick cuddle. "Of

course you can. But you can't do any magic. I have to do this all by myself. Deal?"

Flame nodded seriously.

Mrs. Watson came out to give her a hug and wish her good luck.

"Thanks, Mom. See you later," Jemma said.

As she set off down the street, she began to sing her song to herself. But after the first line, she stopped. She couldn't seem to remember any of the steps. Maybe they'd come to her if she concentrated on her routine. But it was no use. The whole thing seemed jumbled up in her mind.

A terrible, uncomfortable feeling crept up on Jemma. Her stomach churned and her knees began shaking. The thought of facing the panel of judges filled her with sudden panic.

"It's no use, Flame. I thought I could do this, but I can't!" she burst out.

Flame looked up at her and whimpered softly.

Jemma stopped, trying to decide what to do. She couldn't bear to go home and face her mom's disappointment, but there was no way she could face Fran either.

Crossing the street, she started walking quickly, with no idea of where she was going.

Flame walked along beside her in silence as they wove through the streets, then as they turned a corner he suddenly bounded ahead.

"Jemma, come!" Flame instructed as he purposefully made his way across the

road and through some tall, decorative
iron gates.

Jemma looked up in surprise. They
were at the park. She hadn't realized how
far she had walked. But where was Flame
going? He had never taken off like that
before.

She quickly checked the road for cars

and then dashed into the park after him.

"Flame! Where are you?" she cried urgently as she jogged across the grass and checked out the flower beds. Then she caught a glimpse of cream and brown fur over by the garbage can, but by the time she got there he was gone again.

When she finally caught up with him by a park bench, she was out of breath. "There you are, Flame! Why did you run off?" she panted, flopping down onto the seat.

"You told me that I was not to do magic," Flame told her, leaping up to crouch beside her. "But I had to help you somehow."

As Jemma stroked the top of Flame's fluffy head, she realized that her attack of nerves had faded. Running after Flame had made her forget all about herself, which was just what he'd planned! She felt much better now. Just to test herself, she went through the routine in her mind. She could remember every single move.

"Will you go to the audition now?" Flame purred hopefully.

"I don't know . . ." Jemma took a deep breath. She thought of Fran waiting there for her and made up her mind. "All right. Let's go!" she said, jumping to her feet. But a quick glance at her watch filled her with dismay. "Oh, no! I'm so late. I'll never get to the town hall in time. Unless . . ." She looked down at Flame. "I know I said you couldn't use magic to help me win, but can you help me get there, please?"

Flame grinned as his fur began glowing with sparks and his whiskers crackled with electricity.

Chapter
EIGHT

Jemma felt a bump as she landed. She was in a stall in a ladies bathroom— wearing her new costume! She could hear lots of nervous voices talking about the auditions. She was inside the town hall.

Opening the door, she poked her head outside. There was a long line of people twisting all down the hallway. Just then, Fran came out of a room, looking hot and breathless.

She rushed right over. "Jemma! Where

have you been? I thought you weren't coming. Quick, it's your turn next. They're waiting for you."

There was no time to explain anything. Fran opened the door and almost pushed Jemma inside.

Jemma's heart pounded as she saw the judges sitting at a long table. She introduced herself and gave them her music tape.

"All right, Jemma. Show us what you can do," one of the judges said with a smile.

Jemma took her starting position.

This was it! All her hard work had brought her here. Her hopes and dreams of going to dance school were relying on the next few minutes.

As the music filled the room, Jemma

began her routine. As she danced, she
forgot to be nervous. The sheer joy of
performing carried her along. She twisted,
jumped, and swayed in time to the beat.

It was going really well until she
missed a step and almost tripped. But in
a split second, she recovered and carried

on as if nothing had happened. She gave a final twirl and finished. Breathing hard, she straightened up.

She searched the judges' faces but couldn't tell what they were thinking.

"Thank you, Jemma. You'll hear from us in a few days." The judges smiled coolly.

She grabbed her tape, thanked the judges politely, and went outside.

Fran was waiting for her. "Well? How did it go?" she asked eagerly.

Jemma's shoulders sagged. "Okay at first, but I made a stupid mistake. I don't think they were very impressed. They didn't say a word about how I did. How about you?"

"The same," Fran said, making a face. "But they told us earlier they didn't have time to discuss the routines. There's too many people to see."

"Really?" Jemma said. Maybe she still had a chance.

But she couldn't convince herself. That mistake had been stupid and clumsy.

Maybe she had been fooling herself to think she could win a place at dance school, anyway.

"How about a barbecue in the garden?" Mrs. Watson suggested the following evening.

"Good idea." Jemma tried to sound enthusiastic. She knew her mom was trying to cheer her up. "Come on, Flame. Let's go and work in the garden."

Mrs. Watson laughed. "I hope that kitten can use a lawn mower!"

Jemma hid a smile as Flame walked into the garden after her. If only her mom knew!

There were some boxes of flowers outside the back door. Her mom had gotten them cheap when the supermarket had a sale, but didn't have time to plant them.

"Maybe I spoke too soon," Jemma sighed as she looked at the tangle of weeds, long grass, and scruffy paving stones. But Flame took one look at it and sparks leaped out of his fur. There was a silver flash! Jemma shut her eyes against the light. When she was sure it was okay again, Jemma slowly opened one eye, holding her breath in anticipation.

The garden was transformed!

The flowers were all planted and the lawn had been mown. The paving stones were in place.

"It's perfect. Mom's going to love it!" she scooped Flame up and buried her face in his soft fur. "Thanks, Flame! I'll tell her I had a lot of help from a friend with the gardening. It's true in a way, isn't it?"

Suddenly Flame stiffened. She felt him begin to tremble.

Jemma frowned. "What's wrong?"

"I sense my enemies close by!" he meowed nervously. "I must go soon! I need to find a new hiding place!"

Jemma felt her stomach clench. She had known this moment would come eventually, but she had never wanted it to. What would she do without Flame? Jemma looked at the trembling kitten and

sighed. She knew she was going to have
to be stronger than this. Flame was in
danger. If his uncle's spies found him, he
would be killed. "You should go, now!"
she forced herself to say.

Flame shook his head. "I must build
up my magic. It takes time."

"You'll be safer in the house." Jemma took him in and ran up the stairs two at a time. "Maybe you could hide inside my closet?"

She made a nest out of some clothes. Flame crept right inside and curled up. His big green eyes and pink nose were all that could be seen. He looked very tiny and vulnerable.

Jemma felt scared for him. A wave of heavy sadness washed over her. First, she had almost definitely lost her chance to go to dance school. Now she was going to lose Flame. She didn't think she could handle it.

"Jems! Mom's got the stuff for the barbecue." Georgie came to get her. "She says I can cook the sausages, if you help me."

"All right, I'm coming." Jemma made a huge effort to push her worries aside. She definitely wasn't hungry anymore. She took a last look at the closet where Flame was hiding and then slowly followed Georgie downstairs.

Jemma didn't sleep well that night. She had nightmares about cats chasing Flame and woke up when it was still dark.

Flame had crept in beside her. She cuddled up to him, feeling terrible. His little furry body was comforting.

"I wish you could stay here forever," she murmured.

"I cannot," Flame meowed sadly. "In my homeland I will be king, one day."

Jemma nodded sadly. "I know."

The next time Jemma woke up, it was time to get up. She was putting on her school uniform when she heard the sound of the mailbox. The mail was here!

When she came into the kitchen, her mom held out an envelope. It was the results from the audition. Any minute now she would know the bad news.

Jemma felt sick. "Will you read it, please, Mom?"

Mrs. Watson opened the letter slowly. As she read, her face changed. "You did it, Jemma! You won a scholarship!"

Jemma's jaw dropped. She couldn't believe it. "Let me see!" She scanned the letter with shining eyes. "They think I'm talented. And they were impressed because I didn't let a small mistake get in the way . . ." She looked up. "Oh, Mom. I did it! I'm going to dance school!"

Mrs. Watson gave her a big hug. "I knew you'd do it! I'm so proud of you, sweetie!"

Jemma had to tell Flame. She almost flew up the stairs.

"Flame, I'm going to dance school!"

she cried, pushing open the door. "I did it, all by myself. And . . . oh!"

There was a bright silver flash. On the rug stood the elegant white lion. Silver sparks glittered in his fur like a thousand fireflies.

Prince Flame! He was no longer in disguise as a cream and brown kitten. Jemma gasped. She had almost forgotten how stunning he was in his true form.

An older-looking gray lion stood next to Prince Flame. "We must hurry, Your Highness," he growled urgently.

"You're leaving right now?" Jemma asked, her voice breaking.

Prince Flame's emerald eyes crinkled as he smiled sadly. "I must. My enemies are getting closer."

Tears came to her eyes. She managed

a shaky smile. "We had a great time, didn't we? I'll never forget you."

She stretched out her hand. Prince Flame lowered his head and allowed her to pet him one last time before he backed away.

"Be good. Be strong, Jemma." He raised a shining white paw in farewell.

Both cats began to fade. There was a final spurt of silver sparks and they were gone.

Jemma wiped her eyes. Something glittered on her bed. It was a single silver sparkle. Reaching out, she picked it up. It tingled against her palm before blinking out.

"Be safe, wherever you go, Prince Flame," she murmured.

Just then she heard a knock on the

front door. An excited voice called through the mailbox. "It's me, Fran! My letter came this morning. I've got great news!"

Jemma took a deep breath as she thought about Flame for a moment longer, then she raced downstairs, a huge grin breaking out on her face.

"So do I!" she shouted.

About the Author

Sue Bentley's books for children often include animals or fairies. She lives in Northampton and enjoys reading, going to the movies, and sitting and watching the frogs and newts in her garden pond. If she hadn't been a writer, she would probably have been a skydiver or a brain surgeon. The main reason she writes is that she can drink pots and pots of tea while she's typing. She has met and owned many cats and each one has brought a special sort of magic to her life.